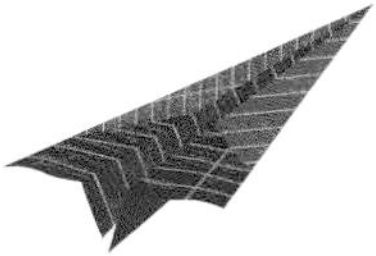

ROALD DAHL'S

SECRET PLANS

working in partnership with

National Literacy Trust

ILLUSTRATED BY QUENTIN BLAKE

PUFFIN

PUFFIN BOOKS

UK | USA | Canada | Ireland | Australia
India | New Zealand | South Africa

Puffin Books is part of the Penguin Random House group of companies
whose addresses can be found at global.penguinrandomhouse.com.

puffinbooks.com

Penguin
Random House
UK

Made for McDonald's 2015
001

Esio Trot: first published in Great Britain by Jonathan Cape 1990
The Twits: first published in Great Britain by Jonathan Cape 1980
Published in paperback by Puffin Books

Printed in Slovakia

A CIP catalogue record for this book is available from the British Library

ISBN: 978–0–141–36255–7

Batch nr.: 123915/16

FSC
MIX
FSC® C022120

Explore the extraordinary world of

ROALD DAHL

Discover the elaborate **secret** plan that MR HOPPY hatches to make Mrs Silver **happy**.

And find out why MR and MRS TWIT are always planning **nasty** tricks to play on each other.

Bring Roald Dahl's extraordinary stories to life with the **Happy Studio** app. Simply download the app to a phone or tablet and read the stories in this book aloud to experience the fun.

Isn't he
gorgeous?

Mr Hoppy's Ingenious Plan
from

ESIO TROT

Alfie the tortoise had been Mrs Silver's adored pet for years and he lived on her balcony summer and winter. Mrs Silver's dearest wish was for Alfie to grow. Mr Hoppy was Mrs Silver's upstairs neighbour and he had been secretly in love with her for years.

'You really *would* love him to grow bigger, wouldn't you?' Mr Hoppy said, and even as he said it his mind suddenly went *click* and an amazing idea came rushing into his head.

'Of course I would!' Mrs Silver cried. 'I'd give *anything* to make it happen!'

Back in his flat, Mr Hoppy was simply quivering all over with excitement.

But there was a lot of work to be done before he could carry out his plan.

The only furniture in Mr Hoppy's small living-room was a table and two chairs. These he moved into his bedroom. Then he went out and bought a sheet of thick canvas and spread it over the entire living-room floor

to protect his carpet.

Next, he got out the telephone-book and wrote down the address of every pet-shop in the city. There were fourteen of them altogether.

It took him two days to visit each pet-shop and choose his tortoises. He wanted a great many, at least one hundred, perhaps more. And he had to choose them very carefully.

To you and me there is not much difference between one tortoise and another. They differ only in their size and in the colour of their shells. Alfie had a darkish shell, so Mr Hoppy chose only the darker-shelled tortoises for his great collection.

Size, of course, was everything. Mr Hoppy chose all sorts of different sizes, some weighing only slightly more than Alfie's thirteen ounces, others a great deal more, but he didn't want any that weighed less.

'Feed them cabbage leaves,' the pet-shop owners told him. 'That's all they'll need. And a bowl of water.'

When he had finished, Mr Hoppy, in his enthusiasm, had bought no less than one hundred and forty tortoises and he carried them home in baskets, ten or fifteen at a time. He had to

make a lot of trips and he was quite exhausted at the end of it all, but it was worth it. Boy, was it worth it! And what an amazing sight his living-room was when they were all in there together! The floor was swarming with tortoises of different sizes, some walking slowly about and exploring, some munching cabbage leaves, others drinking water from a big shallow dish.

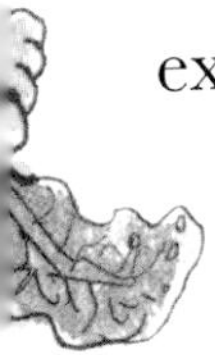

They made just the faintest rustling sound as they moved over the canvas sheet, but that was all. Mr Hoppy had to pick his way carefully on his toes between this moving sea of brown shells whenever he walked across the room. But enough of that. He must get on with the job.

Before he retired Mr Hoppy had been a mechanic in a bus-garage. And now he went back to his old place of work and asked his mates if he might use his old bench for an hour or two.

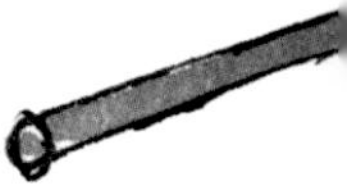

What he had to do now was to make something that would reach down from his own balcony to Mrs Silver's balcony and pick up a tortoise. This was not difficult for a mechanic like Mr Hoppy.

First he made two metal claws or fingers, and these he attached to the end

of a long metal tube. He ran two stiff wires down inside the tube and connected them to the metal claws in such a way that when you pulled the wires, the claws closed, and when you pushed them, the claws opened.

The wires were joined to a handle at the other end of the tube. It was all very simple.

Mr Hoppy was ready to begin.

Mrs Silver had a part-time job. She worked from noon until

five o'clock every weekday afternoon in a shop that sold newspapers and sweets. That made things a lot easier for Mr Hoppy.

So on that first exciting afternoon, after he had made sure that Mrs Silver had gone to work, Mr Hoppy went out on to his balcony armed with his long metal pole. He called this his tortoise-catcher. He leaned over the balcony railings and lowered the pole down on to Mrs Silver's balcony below.

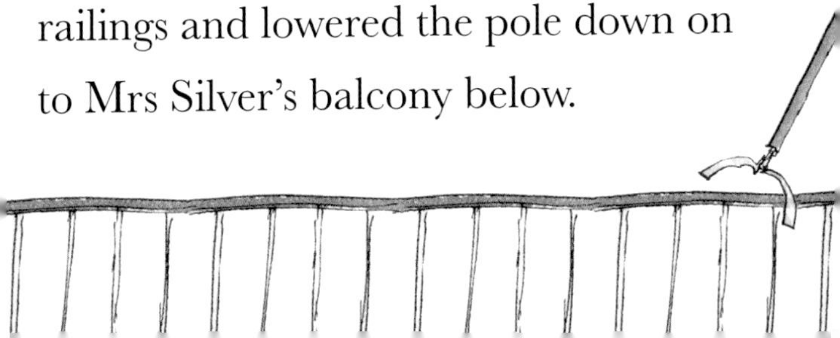

Alfie was basking in the pale sunlight over to one side.

'Hello, Alfie,' Mr Hoppy said. 'You are about to go for a little ride.'

He wiggled the tortoise-catcher till it was right above Alfie. He pushed the hand-lever so that the claws opened wide. Then he lowered the two claws neatly over Alfie's shell and pulled the lever. The claws closed tightly over the shell like two fingers of a hand. He hauled Alfie up on to his own balcony. It was easy.

Mr Hoppy weighed Alfie on his own kitchen scales just to make sure that Mrs Silver's figure of thirteen ounces was correct. It was.

Now, holding Alfie in one hand, he picked his way carefully through his huge collection of tortoises to find one that first of all had the same colour shell as Alfie's and secondly weighed *exactly two ounces more.*

Two ounces is not much. It is less than a smallish hen's egg weighs. But, you see, the important thing in Mr Hoppy's plan was to make sure that the new tortoise was bigger than Alfie but only a *tiny bit* bigger. The difference had to be so small that Mrs Silver wouldn't notice it.

From his vast collection, it was not difficult for Mr Hoppy to find just the tortoise he wanted. He wanted one that weighed fifteen ounces exactly on his kitchen scales, no more and no less.

When he had got it, he put it on the kitchen table beside Alfie, and even he could hardly tell that one was bigger than the other. But it *was* bigger. It was bigger by two ounces. This was Tortoise Number 2.

Mr Hoppy took Tortoise Number 2 out on to the balcony and gripped it in the claws of his tortoise-catcher. Then he lowered it on to Mrs Silver's balcony, right beside a nice fresh lettuce.

Tortoise Number 2 had never eaten tender juicy lettuce leaves before.

It had only had thick old cabbage leaves. It loved the lettuce and started chomping away at it with great gusto.

There followed a rather nervous two hours' wait for Mrs Silver to return from work.

Would she see any difference between the new tortoise and Alfie? It was going to be a tense moment.

Out on to her balcony swept Mrs Silver.

'Alfie, my darling!' she cried out. 'Mummy's back! Have you missed me?'

Mr Hoppy, peering over his railing, but well hidden between two huge potted plants, held his breath.

The new tortoise was still chomping away at the lettuce.

Mr Hoppy popped his head out of the foliage and called out, 'Good evening, Mrs Silver. How is Alfie tonight?'

'Oh, he's lovely,' Mrs Silver said, looking up and beaming. 'And he's developing *such* an appetite! I've never seen him eat like this before!'

As well as his ingenious plan for swapping tortoises, **Mr Hoppy** knows another **extraordinary** secret about them. TORTOISES understand humans when they speak **backwards**! Did you notice that ESIO TROT is 'tortoise' spelled **backwards**?

Can you work out these words, now you know the **secret**?

1 EIFLA

the name of Mrs Silver's pet tortoise

....

2 LLEHS

the dome-shaped part of a tortoise

....

3 EGABBAC

the vegetable that Mr Hoppy feeds his tortoises

....

4 YNOCLAB

the place where Mr Hoppy grows plants

....

5 TEG REGGIB

what Mrs Silver wants Alfie to do

....

Do you have the **Happy Studio** app downloaded? Launch it **now** for an **extra** activity!

I'm Mr Twit – an extremely **horrid**, old man!
I'm Mrs Twit and I'm **no better** than my husband!

The Frog, the Wormy Spaghetti and the Funny Walking-stick

from

THE TWITS

Mr Twit had a plan for a trick to play on his wife: he would put a frog in Mrs Twit's bed.

He caught a big one down by the pond and carried it back secretly in a box.

That night, when Mrs Twit was in the bathroom getting ready for bed, Mr Twit slipped the frog between her sheets. Then he got into his own bed and waited for the fun to begin.

Mrs Twit came back and climbed into her bed and put out the light.

She lay there in the dark scratching her tummy. Her tummy was itching. Dirty old hags like her always have itchy tummies.

Then all at once she felt something cold and slimy crawling over her feet. She screamed.

'What's the matter with you?' Mr Twit said.

'Help!' screamed Mrs Twit, bouncing about. 'There's something in my bed!'

'I'll bet it's that Giant Skillywiggler I saw on the floor just now,' Mr Twit said.

'That *what*?' screamed Mrs Twit.

'I tried to kill it but it got away,' Mr Twit said. 'It's got teeth like screwdrivers!'

'Help!' screamed Mrs Twit. 'Save me! It's all over my feet!'

'It'll bite off your toes,' said Mr Twit.

Mrs Twit fainted.

Mr Twit got out of bed and fetched a jug of cold water. He poured the water over Mrs Twit's head to revive her. The frog crawled up from under the sheets to get near the water. It started jumping about on the pillow. Frogs love water. This one was having a good time.

When Mrs Twit came to, the frog had just jumped on to her face. This is not a nice thing to happen to anyone in bed at night. She screamed again.

'By golly it *is* a Giant Skillywiggler!' Mr Twit said. 'It'll bite off your nose.'

Mrs Twit leapt out of bed and flew downstairs and spent the night on the sofa. The frog went to sleep on her pillow.

The next day, to pay Mr Twit back for the frog trick, Mrs Twit sneaked out into the garden and dug up some worms. She chose big long ones and put them in a tin and carried the tin back to the house under her apron.

At one o'clock, she cooked spaghetti for lunch and she mixed the worms in with the spaghetti, but only on her husband's plate. The worms didn't show because everything was covered with tomato sauce and sprinkled with cheese.

'Hey, my spaghetti's moving!' cried Mr Twit, poking around in it with his fork.

'It's a new kind,' Mrs Twit said, taking a mouthful from her own plate which of course had no worms. 'It's called Squiggly Spaghetti. It's delicious. Eat it up while it's nice and hot.'

Mr Twit started eating, twisting the long tomato-covered strings around his fork and shovelling them into his mouth. Soon there was tomato sauce all over his hairy chin.

'It's not as good as the ordinary kind,' he said, talking with his mouth full. 'It's too squishy.'

'I find it very tasty,' Mrs Twit said. She was watching him from the other end of the table. It gave her great pleasure to watch him eating worms.

'I find it rather bitter,' Mr Twit said. 'It's got a distinctly bitter flavour. Buy the other kind next time.'

Mrs Twit waited until Mr Twit had eaten the whole plateful. Then she said, 'You want to know why your spaghetti was squishy?'

Mr Twit wiped the tomato sauce from his beard with a corner of the tablecloth. 'Why?' he said.

'And why it had a nasty bitter taste?'

'Why?' he said.

'Because it was *worms*!' cried Mrs Twit, clapping her hands and stamping her feet on the floor and rocking with horrible laughter.

To pay Mrs Twit back for the worms in his spaghetti, Mr Twit thought up a really clever nasty trick.

One night, when the old woman was asleep, he crept out of bed and took her walking-stick downstairs to his workshed. There he stuck a tiny round piece of wood (no thicker than a penny) on to the bottom of the stick.

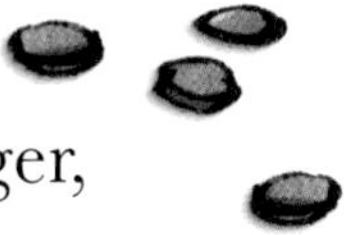

This made the stick longer, but the difference was so small the next morning Mrs Twit didn't notice it.

The following night, Mr Twit stuck on another tiny bit of wood. Every

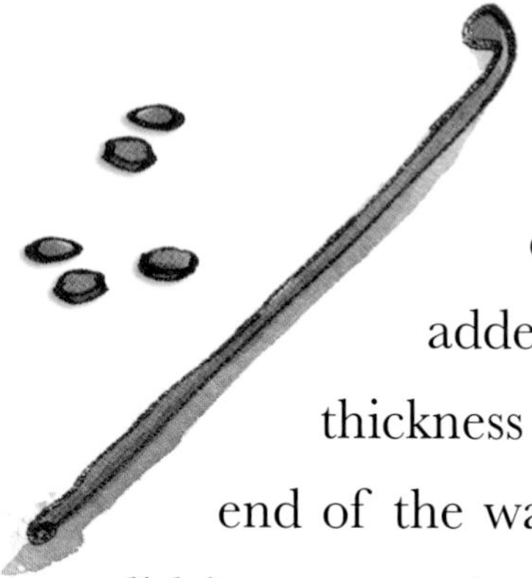

night, he crept downstairs and added an extra tiny thickness of wood to the end of the walking-stick. He did it very neatly so that the extra bits looked like a part of the old stick.

Gradually, but oh so gradually, Mrs Twit's walking-stick was getting longer and longer.

Now when something is growing very slowly, it is almost impossible to notice it happening. You yourself, for example, are actually growing taller every day that goes by, but you wouldn't think it, would you? It's happening so slowly you can't even notice it from one week to the next.

It was the same with Mrs Twit's walking-stick. It was all so slow and gradual that she didn't notice how long it was getting even when it was halfway up to her shoulder.

'That stick's too long for you,' Mr Twit said to her one day.

'Why so it is!' Mrs Twit said, looking at the stick. 'I've had a feeling there was something wrong but I couldn't for the life of me think what it was.'

'There's something wrong all right,' Mr Twit said, beginning to enjoy himself.

'What *can* have happened?' Mrs Twit said, staring at her old walking-stick. 'It must suddenly have grown longer.'

'Don't be a fool!' Mr Twit said. 'How can a walking-stick possibly grow longer? It's made of dead wood, isn't it? Dead wood can't grow.'

'Then what on earth has happened?' cried Mrs Twit.

'It's not the stick, it's *you*!' said Mr Twit, grinning horribly. 'It's *you* that's getting *shorter*! I've been noticing it for some time now.'

'That's not true!' cried Mrs Twit.

'You're shrinking, woman!' said Mr Twit.

'It's not possible!'

'Oh yes it jolly well is,' said Mr Twit. 'You're shrinking fast! You're shrinking *dangerously* fast! Why, you must have shrunk at least a foot in the last few days!'

'Never!' she cried.

'Of course you have! Take a look at your stick, you old goat, and see how much you've shrunk in comparison! You've got the *shrinks*, that's what you've got! You've got the dreaded *shrinks*!'

Mrs Twit began to feel so trembly she had to sit down.

As soon as Mrs Twit sat down, Mr Twit pointed at her and shouted, 'There you are! You're sitting in your old chair and you've shrunk so much your feet aren't even touching the ground!'

Mrs Twit looked down at her feet and by golly the man was right. Her feet were not touching the ground.

Mr Twit, you see, had been just as clever with the chair as he'd been with the walking-stick. Every night when he had gone downstairs and stuck a little bit extra on to the stick, he had done the same to the four legs of Mrs Twit's chair.

'Just look at you sitting there in your same old chair,' he cried, 'and you've shrunk so much your feet are dangling in the air!'

Mrs Twit went white with fear.

'You've got the *shrinks*!' cried Mr Twit, pointing his finger at her like a pistol. 'You've got them badly! You've got the most terrible case of shrinks I've ever seen!'

Mrs Twit became so frightened she began to dribble. But Mr Twit, still remembering the worms in his spaghetti, didn't feel sorry for her at all. 'I suppose you know what *happens* to you when you get the shrinks?' he said.

'What?' gasped Mrs Twit. 'What happens?'

'Your head SHRINKS into your neck . . .

'And your neck SHRINKS into your body . . .

'And your body SHRINKS into your legs . . .

'And your legs SHRINK into your feet. And in the end there's nothing left except a pair of shoes and a bundle of old clothes.'

'I can't bear it!' cried Mrs Twit.

'It's a terrible disease,' said Mr Twit.

'The worst in the world.'

'How long have I got?' cried Mrs Twit. 'How long before I finish up as a bundle of old clothes and a pair of shoes?'

Mr Twit put on a very solemn face. 'At the rate you're going,' he said, shaking his head sadly, 'I'd say not more than ten or eleven days.'

'But isn't there *anything* we can do?' cried Mrs Twit.

'There's only one cure for the shrinks,' said Mr Twit.

'Tell me!' she cried. 'Oh, tell me quickly!'

'We'll have to hurry!' said Mr Twit.

'I'm ready. I'll hurry! I'll do anything you say!' cried Mrs Twit.

'You won't last long if you don't,' said Mr Twit, giving her another grizzly grin.

'What is it I must do?' cried Mrs Twit, clutching her cheeks.

'You've got to be *stretched*,' said Mr Twit.

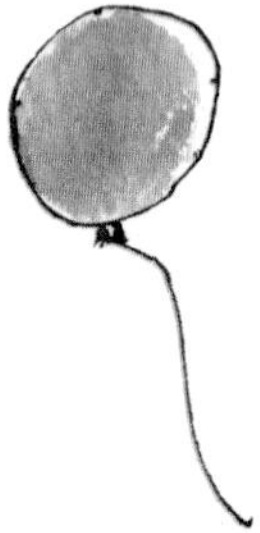

When Mr Twit secretly **lengthens** Mrs Twit's walking-stick, she thinks she has got the **shrinks**.

Can you draw yourself with the shrinks?

Do you have the **Happy Studio** app downloaded? Launch it **now** for an **extra** activity!